T0198789

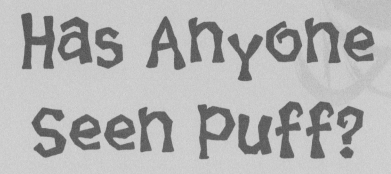

Has Anyone Seen Puff?

A Billy and Jake Adventure

SHERI WOLFINGER

Order this book online at www.trafford.com
or email orders@trafford.com

Most Trafford titles are also available at major online book retailers.

 www.trafford.com

North America & international
toll-free: 844 688 6899 (USA & Canada)
fax: 812 355 4082

Our mission is to efficiently provide the world's finest, most comprehensive book publishing service, enabling every author to experience success. To find out how to publish your book, your way, and have it available worldwide, visit us online at www.trafford.com

Illustrated by Brandi Wolfinger

ISBN: 978-1-4669-1377-6 (sc)
ISBN: 978-1-4669-5317-8 (e)

Library of Congress Control Number: 2012902722

Print information available on the last page.

Trafford rev. 03/19/2021

Advanced readers should read the text at the tops of the pages.

This is an original "2-in-1" book. The book that will grow with your child's reading ability. Beginner readers should read the text at the bottoms of the pages. More advanced readers should be reading the text at the tops of the pages. The book will not only grow with your child but teach good morals through the silly adventures of Billy and Jake. Look for upcoming Billy and Jake adventure tales.

Beginner readers should read the easy text at the bottoms of the pages.

A Billy and Jake Adventure

Has Anyone Seen Puff?

Written by Sheri Wolfinger

Illustrated by Brandi Wolfinger

Every day was an adventure on the Kokomos' farm. They had lots of animals, and two very adventurous pups. Their names were Billy and Jake.

Everyone that knew the Kokomos heard of Billy & Jake, and their mischief. They didn't look for trouble. It just seemed to find them. Billy was okay on his own, but Jake was too curious for his own good. When they teamed up, watch out!

The Kokomos had two puppies. Their names were Billy and Jake.

People said that the Kokomos kept the puppies because of their mother. She had been part of the Kokomo family since she had been a pup. Five years earlier, she showed up on their porch, half-starved to death, with the tip of her tail missing. She was called Tippy since that day. No one was sure if it had been snipped off or bitten. It was just gone. No one knew where she came from, but she earned her keep as a great watchdog. Many times, Tippy chased wild animals from the farm and foxes from the hen house. Mr. Kokomo would always say, "Yep, she's a keeper alright." The only thing that Tippy had in mind was to protect the family that she loved so much.

Their mother was the Kokomos' watchdog. Her name was Tippy.

Tippy scolded Billy and Jake time and time again. She tried to convince her pups how lucky they were. She would say, "You should be thankful for a place to sleep, food to eat and people to care for you." Tippy remembered hard times when she did not have such a good life. She told her pups someday the Kokomos would get tired of their shenanigans, and give them to the first passerby.

Billy and Jake were very naughty. Well mostly Jake was very naughty.

She didn't truly believe what she said. She was just trying to keep her young pups out of trouble. Of course she wasn't talking like you or I. It sounded more like, "Ruff, ruff, arf, woof, woof, arf, ruff, bark!" She spoke in animal language so only the animals could understand. No person knew the pups were being scolded by their mother. It just sounded like Tippy was making a lot of noise.

Their mother often had to scold them.

Let me tell you of one of the not-so-unusual days on the farm.

It was a beautiful warm day; Mr. Kokomo had just finished milking old Betsy, the cow. He set the pail of milk on the ground for only a minute. One minute was long enough. Then it happened. Puff, the barn cat, poked her head around the corner. She did not see Jake sunning himself in the doorway of the barn. Puff sneaked over to the pail of milk very, very, very slowly. She just about had her little tongue in the milk when Jake opened his eyes. He spotted Puff. Then everything happened very fast!

Mr. Kokomo milked old Betsy the cow. Puff tried to steal some of the milk.

Jake wasn't too concerned about protecting the milk. He was more worried about the fact that Puff was getting something that he was not getting. Oh my, jealousy can cause all sorts of problems. He took off after Puff like a cat after a mouse. Puff ran around the pail with Jake close behind her. The pail got knocked and splashed a little bit. Everything may have turned out okay except Mr. Kokomo tried to chase them from the barn. They were upsetting the other animals. Well I guess that you could say that Mr. Kokomo kicked the bucket. Almost an entire pail of milk splashed up and all over him. He was very upset. He did succeed in getting the fight out of the barn. Puff ran for the protection of Mrs. Kokomo.

Jake chased Puff. Mr. Kokomo chased Jake. The milk pail spilled.

Puff was running from Jake and the shouting Mr. Kokomo. Puff was going so fast, and was so scared, that she missed Mrs. Kokomo coming around the corner of the henhouse with a full basket of eggs. It was not full for long. She tripped over Puff and lost her balance. She fell into the only mud puddle between the henhouse and the porch. There sat Mrs. Kokomo, covered in mud and broken eggs, with Mr. Kokomo running to her in milk soaked pants. What a site! That did not stop Jake. If it didn't stop Jake, it didn't stop Puff. The race continued.

Mrs. Kokomo tripped over Puff. She fell into a mud puddle and broke the eggs.

Puff knew that she couldn't stop and Jake knew that he wouldn't stop. Jake was thinking that he would keep going until he caught that furry, little, milk stealing cat! They went tearing around the corner of the house. Puff spotted an opened window and jumped for it. It was a wonderful jump! It was a jump to be proud of except . . . . . . the jump landed her with her paws in a fresh blueberry pie that had been sitting by the window to cool. She knew she was in BIG trouble! There would be no acting innocent either with little blue-violet paw prints which trailed across the kitchen floor. The second that the muddy Mrs. Kokomo opened the door Puff ran outside. She never paused until she was safely hidden inside the barn.

Puff jumped in the window and into a pie. She ran to the barn to hide.

Meanwhile, Jake was just leaving his place outside the opened window, where he had been waiting for Puff to reappear. He was growling, "She got away this time. Next time I will get that cat." During all of the excitement, Billy was looking for his mother. He found Tippy and she was very upset. When Jake saw her step around the corner, all he could say was, "uh oh."

Jake waited for Puff at the window.

"Uh, oh does not begin to describe the trouble that you are in this time Jake," his mother announced. He was in BIG trouble and he knew it. This was almost as bad as the time that he chased the skunk in through the front door of the house and right out the back. No one forgot about that for weeks or possibly months. It was stinky! The odor seemed to last forever but that is another story to tell.

Jake remembered the last time that he was in big trouble. It was when he chased a skunk into the house.

Jake's mother really scolded him this time. He was not allowed to leave the front yard for two whole weeks. He thought that was not too bad. Then his mother said, "No table scraps for just as long too!" Oh that was big punishment. He loved table scraps. The pups always had food but nothing was as good as the leftover table scraps. They were a real treat when they got them! The idea of missing out if there were scraps was a terrible thought. He made it through two weeks of punishment staying out of trouble most of the time. Puff did enjoy teasing him very much during his punishment.

Jake was not allowed special treats for two weeks. He also was not to leave the front yard for two weeks.

Trouble continued to happen around Jake. Like I said before, he didn't look for trouble, it just found him. But as Jake grew older he began to learn from his mistakes. He started to listen to his mother's talks instead of just wanting them to be over. He finally learned that one of two things can happen with trouble. It can be avoided or it can happen. He started to learn how to avoid it. He grew up to be a great watchdog, just like his mother. He and Billy became so loved by the Kokomos that they laugh when they talk about the mischief the pups caused in their younger, early dog days.

Billy and Jake listened to their mother. They grew up to become great watchdogs.

Remember the lessons that Jake learned the hard way. Jealousy is a terrible thing and trouble doesn't have to happen. Think before you act and there should be some way to avoid it.

Special thanks to some special friends for listening to their parents.

Jeremy Aaron		Steffanie Ara
Carley Aaron	Caitlyn Marie	Jillian Lee
Alexis Ara		Aliveah Neveah
David Nathaniel		Kaitlyn Nichole
Sara Elizabeth		Brantley David

Listen to your parents. They will teach you.

Look for upcoming Billy and Jake adventures.

<u>The Funny Black and White Cat</u> – A Billy and Jake Adventure

Printed in the United States
by Baker & Taylor Publisher Services